George B. Rose, George B. Rose

Sebastian : a dramatic poem

George B. Rose, George B. Rose

Sebastian : a dramatic poem

ISBN/EAN: 9783743302884

Manufactured in Europe, USA, Canada, Australia, Japa

Cover: Foto ©Andreas Hilbeck / pixelio.de

Manufactured and distributed by brebook publishing software
(www.brebook.com)

George B. Rose, George B. Rose

Sebastian : a dramatic poem

SEBASTIAN

A DRAMATIC POEM

BUFFALO
CHARLES WELLS MOULTON
1894

DRAMATIS PERSONAE.

SEBASTIAN.

LALAGE.

POLYCARP, an old man, husband to Lalage.

ANTONIO,
FELIX, } Friends to Sebastian.

OROSIUS,
PETRONIUS, } Professors in the University.

A PRIEST.

SEBASTIAN.

SCENE I.

Sebastian Alone.   Enter Priest.

PRIEST.

Good morning, son.

SEBASTIAN.

   Good morning, holy father, pray
Be seated.

PRIEST.

How is my son to-day?

SEBASTIAN.

Why, well, your reverence, well as one can be
Wrapped in the shadow of so great a grief.

PRIEST.

I would, my son, point out the one relief.
There is but One who can give consolation,
There is but One with power to lift us up,
Sweetening the contents of the bitter cup,
And bringing peace to those in desolation.
Hast thou sought aid from him?

SEBASTIAN.

I have, my father, but the cup of woe
Is full even to the brim,
And peace I have not found.

PRIEST.

Dispair not, son, the Holy One was crowned
With thorns, and bent beneath the cruel blow;
Yea, perished on the cross that we might gain
Our soul's salvation.   Shall we then complain,
We who have suffered so much less than He?

SEBASTIAN.

Oh! father, father, I recall so well
My days of childhood, when I sought God's shrine
With my poor sainted mother, and when we
Knelt down in prayer together.   Then was mine
The ecstacy of faith.   The deep toned-bell
Rang from the lofty spire as an appeal
Of God to men, and at each mighty stroke
New raptures in my thrilling breast awoke.
The incense floated on the mystic air,
And music seemed from heaven itself to steal
In scarce heard accents, then to swell and swell,
Resounding through the aisles, dim lighted, vast,
And through the pointed arches far above.
My soul was filled with ecstacy of prayer,
And seemed to float away on wings of love
Even till the bounds of this poor earth were passed,

And I could almost see the gates of heaven.
And when amid the perfumed clouds that curled
From swinging censers and the awful hush
Of kneeling worshipers was lifted up
The blood of Him whose life for us was given
I felt my soul borne upward from this world;
And gazing fervently upon the cup
Of blood-changed wine I felt the burning gush
Of tears that flowed from my rapt upturned eyes
In gratitude to Him who Paradise
And all its joys had left to save my soul.
Then Faith dwelt undisturbed within my breast,
But later Doubt a furtive entrance stole,
And now hath almost pushed her from the nest.
When in the sacred shrine I stand again
And hear again the organ's awful roll,
The ancient impulse doth again return,
And for the spirit-life again I yearn.
But Doubt comes back, and with a leaden chain
Doth check my spirit's flight. My soul aspires
To the Ideal, to bright realms above
Bathed in the radiance of celestial love.
At times I seem to hear the angel quires
Singing the praise of Him to whom the earth
Is but a footstool, but the song expires
In slowly fading accents. Since the woe
That robbed me of the man who gave me birth,
I strive in vain to hear the heavenly song;

My feeble soul has sunk beneath the blow,
All vanished from my sight the Seraph throng.

PRIEST.

My son, to the ideal ever cling.
That only keeps the soul above the mire
Of common earth.   Still let thy soul aspire,
Soaring toward heaven on wide-extended wing.
The part of man that lifts him from the brutes,
That makes him worthily the son of God,
Till he can comprehend God's attributes,
Can follow where the blest apostles trod,
It is the soul, the love of the ideal,
The love of something better than the real,
The aspiration toward a higher sphere
Than is vouchsafed to man while dwelling here.
Cling still to that, my son, and when thou feelest
The light within grow faint, kneel down in prayer,
And He to whom in vain thou ne'er appealest
In thy dim lighted closet will be there.

SEBASTIAN.

Father, last night I watched beside the bier
Of him I loved so well.   Upon my knees,
In agony of grief, with many a tear,
I turned to God with supplicating pleas,
Praying most earnestly for the repose
Of his great soul, and that I might not be
Unworthy of his virtues.   Then I arose

As the gray dawn was breaking, but I found
No angel band had come to comfort me,
No peace within the chambers of my breast
But only sorrow, bitter and profound,
My soul dragged down to earth and sore oppressed.
My spirit soared not heavenward on the wings
Of that long, tortured prayer, but dull as lead,
To earthly pain and grief alone it clings,
To hopeless mourning for the noble dead.

PRIEST.

My son, 'tis often thus.   Man's soul is weak,
And often sinks beneath the weight of pain;
But God still reigns, and if His throne we seek
With steadfast purpose it is found again.
Be not discouraged; turn again to Him,
He is not deaf, thy prayer will yet be heard;
And He will take away, oh, trust His word,
The bitter cup now full unto the brim.
But now, my son, I must perforce depart;
God's blessing rest with thee, His peace be in thy heart.

SCENE II.

Sebastian.   Enter Orosius and Petronius.

SEBASTIAN.

Why, enter, learned sirs, in truth I deem
Myself much honored by your presence here.

OROSIUS.

Thy father was a friend held ever dear,
And one of highest ranks in our esteem.
We therefore haste to call upon his son
And to express our sorrow for thy loss.

SEBASTIAN.

I thank you honored sirs, most kindly it is done.
When man's weak spirit bends beneath the cross
The sympathy of others buoys him up,
And helps him bear his burden.   Deeply then
I thank you for a kindness rare in men
Of such distinction.   'Tis the hour to sup,
And I entreat you, come into the hall
Now left so desolate since he is gone,
And there I trust ye gently will recall
His many virtues, and will tell me all
Ye can of him.

OROSIUS.

                    To this we both are drawn
By loving recollection of the days
Of close companionship.   To speak the praise
Of those whose souls have passed beyond the reach
Of mortal envy is a pleasing thing
Even to the jealous.   Gladly then our speech
Will turn to him, for pleasing memories spring
At slightest thought of him.

SEBASTIAN.

Be seated, sirs, and let this ancient wine
In which so oft your friendship he has pledged,
Pressed in his boyhood from the purple vine,
Be poured, a sad libation to his shade.
I do esteem myself most privileged
To speak of him with you.

PETRONIUS.

And 'tis to us a pleasure
To talk with thee, who, now that he is laid
In lasting sleep, dost hold his honored place.

SEBASTIAN.

But so unworthily.   I know the measure
Of his high virtues I can never fill.
He was so calm, of such unbending will,
So self contained, of such majestic grace,
While I am ever weakly passionate.

PETRONIUS.

Thou only comprehendest him when he
Was well advanced in honors and in years,
When through experience and bitter tears
He had acquired the strength to dominate
His bosom's weakness.   But 'tis long that we
Were his companions, and in days of youth
He was much as thou seemest now, in truth.
He then was passionate and overbold,

Loving intensely, somewhat quick to anger,
A spirit much too strong to be controlled,
Fervid in action, yielding then to languor,
And loving dalliance when the task was done.
In short, he then was young, and he was one
To lead in all things, whether good or ill.
'Twas years perfected him ; the flight of time,
Labor, endurance, sorrow, even sin,
Had raised him up unto those heights sublime
Where man his highest mission may fulfill.

SEBASTIAN.

Sin ! what meanest thou ?

PETRONIUS.

     'Twas sin I meant.
He was no painted saint upon a wall,
He was a man ; he proudly entered in,
And plucked the fruit of knowledge with resolve
To be in all a man, to know it all,
And drain the cup of mortal bliss and pain.
And know, young man, that, sad as 'tis to say,
Sin is a path by which we oft attain
That knowledge of ourselves that points the way
To self-control and wisdom which absolve
By noble deeds the errors of the past.
Think'st thou that Adam ere he was out cast
From Paradise was much above the brute ?
At most he was a child whose innocence

Was want of knowledge, guiltless of offence
But as a soulless creature.   When the fruit
Forbidden he had plucked he then became
A man, he comprehended right from wrong,
And when towards noble ends with spirit strong
And earnest love of good and steadfast aim
He struggled on, he first became divine.
Such was thy father.   In his youth's hot glow
He plucked forbidden fruit, and largely drank
Of all the pleasures nature can bestow,
And drained unto the lees life's ruddy wine.
But though he sinned, his spirit never sank,
Never became contaminate and vile,
And knowing all, he chose the better part,
Cleaving to that with great and steadfast heart.

OROSIUS.

Too much thou dost exalt the power for good
That sometimes lies in sin.   When men defile
Their souls with sinning, they instead but find
That they have lost the ardent, lofty mind
Bearing them upward, that it drags them down
Into the mire, till when at length they would
Yet save themselves they find the effort vain
And in the slough of vice dishonored drown.
'Tis true that knowledge is a gem of price,
But woe to him who seeketh it in vice.

PETRONIUS.

'Twas sin I said, not vice, and I admit
That they are few who are not wrecked by it ;
But they the noblest are of all our race
Who have looked earth's temptations in the face,
Have viewed the vales of sweetest dalliance,
Then turned their backs, determined to advance
Upon the upward path. They have a force,
A comprehension of all mortal things,
Enabling them to move upon their course
With more majestic stride than he who clings
Too much to thoughts of timid purity.
I do not mean your father had committed
Faults worthy lasting blame, but benefited
By close acquaintance with all human things
He had attained a grand maturity
That fitted him to be the surest guide
Through all the perils that in life betide.

OROSIUS.

I deem thee still at fault, nor can believe
That sin can aid man's true development.
'Tis sorrow bringeth strength, self-government
And deep reflection. Not in vain we grieve.
Repentance sometimes follows after sin,
And with it sorrow, and we thus may gain
Some good from guilt, but vaster far the loss.

PETRONIUS.

Knowledge of life and sorrow are the things
Essential to man's greatness.   These sin brings
To those repenting deeply.   When the dross
Is melted all away, the metal shines
Far brighter than when virgin from the mines.
If in the crucible we cast coarse stone,
It cracks and bursts and crumbles into dust,
But if instead auriferous ore is thrown
The pure gold issues undefiled by rust.
So 'tis with men; temptation wrecks the base,
But elevates the noble.

OROSIUS.

Still I think
Thou art in error.   We receive the soul
Pure from its Maker.   It should ever shrink
From all contamination, lest the trace
Be left upon its garments.   So they taught,
The mighty ones of old who deeply thought,
Teaching the wisdom of true self-control.
And now, Sebastian, let me say to thee
That in this time of sorrow thou wilt find
Much in the ancient writings to console
The grief that prays upon thy troubled mind.
And three especially I recommend:
The bondman Epictetus who beneath
The slave's coarse garments and the bloody lash

Maintained a lofty soul that would not bend,
A spirit still erect and grandly free;
And him who sadly wore the victor's wreath,
And knew of empire nothing but its cares,
The student passing life amid the clash
Of hostile armies and perfidious snares,
The last, the purest, noblest Antonine
Whose death marked the beginning of decline
For the bright glory of imperial Rome;
Then Seneca, whose prosperous life was spent
In wealth and office, but who met his fate
With dauntless courage when the tyrant sent
The messenger of death.   Now cultivate
Acquaintance with these three.   The ancient tome
Take from the shelf, and thou wilt find relief
Within its pages in this hour of grief.
From them who, whether on the dizzy throne
To which the supplicating nations bowed,
Or fed along with dogs upon a bone,
A slave unnoticed mid the servile crowd,
Maintained the spotless candor of the soul
Thou wilt find much to strengthen and console.

SEBASTIAN.

These have I noticed on my father's shelves,
And somewhat through their pages I have glanced,
Reading how men should fortify themselves
By inward calm against external wrong.

Yet in this hour of grief I have not chanced
To think of them; but now at thy suggestion
I will go seek them, and I make no question
They will assist me to be calm and strong.

PETRONIUS.

There are no nobler writers than those three,
None who in moments of adversity
Bring truer comfort to the troubled soul,
And thou wilt find in them much consolation;
But when thou hast recovered self-control,
Thou wouldst do well to seek for recreation
In other reading.   While the stoic school
Surpasses all in teaching man to rule
His inner weakness, yet 'tis suited better
To those who suffer than to those who act.
When Roman tyrants sought men's minds to fetter
As they had bound their bodies to the rack,
The stoic shone supremely, proudly great.
But for the time of action 'tis not fit.
The Epicurean Cæsar far surpassed
Cato in power to wreck or save the state.
The stoic thinks too much about the last
Sad hour of life to view the rest aright.
He scorns too much our short but keen delight.
In black for him the book of life is writ.
Too much the stoic broods; he can not mingle
Well with the world, and shape it to his ends.

Not in seclusion does a man attain
His full development.   When he contends
In life's fierce conflict, then it is his brain
Acquires a disciplined and supple force
Impossible to him who dwelleth single,
Nor mixes with his fellows.   Life should be
Active and vigilant.   The sad recluse
Whose days are spent in striving to maintain
His own soul's purity from contact coarse
With men of baser nature is not he
Who best fulfils man's mission.   Ships that rest
Forever in the haven may be clean,
But are of little use; while those that breast
The foaming billows of the raging main,
Struggling with desperate courage 'gainst the storm,
Though they with shattered rigging may careen
Before the tempest's fury yet conform
To their true purpose.   For the hour of sorrow
The stoic's sad philosophy is best.
From its stern tenets we the strength may borrow
To meet the worst; but 'tis not well to choose
That system for the guidance of our lives.
To suffer well is much, but he who strives
With earnest resolution is the man
Who doth discharge his duties best.   In action
Should life be passed, and not in vain abstraction.

OROSIUS.

Again we differ, and it seem we can

In naught agree.   To me it seemeth clear
The stoic with his constant fortitude
And self-dominion, of a mind imbued
With earnest principles, for a career
Of active effort is the best prepared.

PETRONIUS.

The trouble is the stoics have not cared
Sufficiently for life to pass it so.

OROSIUS.

Well, now 'tis growing late; 'tis time to go.
Bend not Sebastian, 'neath the weight of woe.
Within brief space we shall again be here;
Well in the meantime mayest thou have fared.

SCENE III.

Sebastian alone in the library.

SEBASTIAN.

My books, ye mock me as ye there are ranged
In comely order on the painted shelves,
Purple and red and green and funeral black.
What is your lesson? I have read and read
Until my soul was sick, my eyes were seared,
And I have seen the wretchedness of man
Even from the day when first to earth he came,
Struggling for life with monsters that are dead,

Until this hour, when, polished, civilized,
He strolls through palaces and marble halls.
Yea, I have read and poured into your depths,
But ye are powerless to satisfy
The craving for I know not what that burns
Ceaseless within my soul, the discontent,
The restless weariness of mortal things,
The aspiration toward an unknown goal,
The unnamed longings that disturb my peace.
And there are times when I would burn you all,
And wander, Cain like, through the desert waste,
Free from the trammels of our modern life,
A savage with my hand 'gainst every man,
Seeking in blood and conflicts and in wild
Indulgence of all passions to forget
The emptiness of life.   And there are times
When I do love you as my children fair,
Turning your pages with intense delight,
Finding each craving satisfied in you.
And then the mood is changed, and ye but mock
The restlessness that grows within my breast,
When even the mighty poets can not bring,
With all their beauty, passion, and distress,
Content to me who read.   Oh happy they
Who are not tortured by this ceaseless strife,
This fondness for all learning, and this love
For that which learning never can supply.
And now to-night ye mock me bitterly.

Ye have no message for my troubled soul.
Ye can not satisfy the wild desires,
The yearnings for a something all unknown,
For life more passionate and more intense,
For pleasure fierce and agonizing pain,
That struggle in my heart.   Ye mock me now,
And I would leave you and would wander forth
I know not where — alas, I know not where.

A knock.   Come in!

Enter Antonio and Felix.

                  Why, can it be?
Why, I am truly glad to see
You once again my worthy friends.

   ANTONIO.

But just returned, we visit you
Whom we are told now make amends
In constant study for the days
Once spent in very different ways.

   SEBASTIAN.

That I have greatly changed is true.
The awful loss I have sustained
Has altered me.   But whence come you?

   ANTONIO.

Felix from Rome, from Paris I.
Five years at Rome has he remained

In constant study of his art,
While I have lived right merrily
In Paris, Mammon's matchless mart.
With deepest sorrow we have learned
Of your affliction.   Scarce returned,
We come with friendly sympathy
To clasp your hand and to express
Our sorrow at your deep distress.

SEBASTIAN.

I thank you, friends; you understand
How great my grief, because you knew
My father and how kind and true
He ever was.

ANTONIO.

            Most truly grand;
Thoughtful and proud, he seemed to spurn
Men's weaknesses; a little stern
His countenance until he smiled,
And then it beamed so sweet and mild,
He seemed transfigured.

FELIX.

            I remember
Only the smile.   When I was poor
I sat one day in bleak December
In my bare room with immature,
Uncertain efforts to give form

To my conceptions.   Fierce the storm
Outside was raging.   Hungry, cold,
My fingers numb, I strove in vain
To give them shape, and from my hold
The pencil slipped.   In blank dispair
I sat while through my dizzy brain
Visions of penury and pain
Were floating   Then upon the stair
There was a step, and he came in.
I only knew him as a man
Of highest place, and when within
My garret I beheld him, I
Was scared.   He spoke, and then began
My poor unfinished sketch to scan.
Long looked he, then he laid it by
To see my pictures on the wall.
Right closely he examined all,
Then turned and said, " These plainly show
That you have talent, but you need
Instruction.   You must learn to know
The masters' works, and to succeed
The technic skill you must acquire.
To-morrow morning come and see
My pictures, and they will inspire
A just ambition, and then we
Will talk about your future.   I
Meanwhile this Magdalen will buy."
And then he laid upon the table

A little pile of coinéd gold,
The picture's price a thousand fold.
All overcome, I scarce was able
To speak and earnestly protest
Against such payment, but he pressed
My hand and said, "Just now perhaps
The picture is not worth the sum,
But when the fleeting years shall lapse,
And days of honored fame shall come,
It will be precious." Saying so,
He kindly smiled and turned to go.
    Next morning I myself presented
All awed and timid at his door,
The rich-carved pannels studying o'er;
And of my boldness near repented
When I was led through lofty halls
With richest hangings on the walls.
At length I stood abashed before
Your father, but he welcomed me
As one that he was glad to see.
He led me to his gallery
Where there were many pictures wrought
By master hands. I had not thought
Such things existed, had not dreamed
Of beauty such as on me beamed
In that enchanted shrine. My soul
Was filled with ecstacy. I gazed
In rapt attention, all amazed,

And free among those gems to stroll.
When I had looked till I was drunk
With beauty, he conducted me
Into the dining hall.   I shrunk
From such magnificence, but he
Bade me be seated.   Then he planned
My course of study, and declared
The means should be at my command.
Now all I am, all I may be
Is due to him.   He has not spared
Money, kind wishes nor advice.
Judge then my agony of woe
To learn his death.   Beneath the blow
My spirit sank.   I knew his price,
And knew full well I never should
Another see so great and good.

SEBASTIAN.

I knew not this.   Since we were boys,
And shared our little pains and joys
I only knew you had devoted
Yourself to art, that you were noted
For pictures in the sacred vein
Which, as men say, almost attain
To Raphæl's heavenly purity.
But every day I hear of deeds
Of kindness by my father done,
And oft I know he planted seeds

That later blossomed in the sun
To flowers of sweetest rarity.
He was indeed a noble tree
That sheltered many 'neath its shade.

FELIX.

From what I learn you seem to be
Absorbed in study.   I'm afraid
These musty books will not console.
For something sweeter pines the soul.
Art only brings unto the heart
A comfort that will not depart.
Come with me back to Rome, to Florence come,
And you will stand transfixed and dumb
Before their treasures.   'Tis the land
Of Italy that bringeth balm
To troubled hearts and rest and calm.
Come, let us seek its golden strand.
Comfort is in its balsamed air
And in its scenes so soft and fair,
Its landscapes bathed in mellow light,
Its azure skies serenely bright,
The gentle contours of its hills,
Its verdant vales where rippling rills
Allure to peaceful meditation
And whisper sweetest consolation.
Come, we will visit churches old
Encrusted all with gleaming gold,

With grand old pictures on the walls
Whose beauty every sense enthralls.
Giotto is there, a genius fresh
As morning breezes, wholesome, strong
In faith, with sympathetic brush
Painting alike the angel throng
And gentle creatures of the fields.
And Fra Angelico, who wields
A pencil dipped in heavens own light,
Showing in colors fair and bright
The very scenes of Paradise,
His faces wrapped in ecstacy,
With softly beaming upturned eyes,
Adoring God's sweet majesty.
And Perugino's charming faces
Where sweetness glows with piety,
And loving soft humility;
And Botticelli's subtle graces,
Bartolomeo's earnest art;
And he, the prince without a peer,
Whose greatness has no counterpart,
Surpassing sweet, yet grand, sublime,
The chiefest master of all time,
In all his glory will appear.
To Italy, oh, come with me,
'Tis there from grief you will be free.

SEBASTIAN.

Since boyhood's days my soul has yearned

For that fair land and in my breast
The wish to visit it has burned,
And robbed me often of my rest.
I will not longer now delay,
But soon together we'll away.

ANTONIO.

Felix is right.   It is distraction
That most you need, and great attraction
Has Italy for all of those
Who seek instruction or repose.
But Felix' views are far from mine
On that which Italy contains
Deserving of our care and pains.
'Tis true I do not like her wine,
But she has women passing fair
Possessed of forms of perfect mould,
Worthy the goddesses of old,
With rounded limbs and bosoms rare
Would make St. Anthony's self grow bold.
Forms so voluptuous scarce are seen
Outside that land, of earth the queen.
And as for art, those vapid saints
Angelico or Giotto paints,
Who 'neath their garments have no limbs,
And can do nothing but sing hyms,
Mere putty dolls that know not passion,
And simper in a saintly fashion,

The true Renaissance they are not.
That was the gladsome strong upheaval
Of men rejoicing in the light,
Escaping from the bitter night
Of long, sad ages mediæval,
And wakening to a happier lot.
It was a re-discovery
Of man's essential dignity
And of the beauty of this earth,
Its love and hope, its joy and mirth.
It was a wakening to the bliss
Of carnal life, of amorous kiss,
Of woman's rich voluptuous charms,
Of plastic limbs and snowy arms,
A glad return to ancient ways,
A yearning for the joyous days
When earth was young and men were glad,
Nor fear of hell had made them sad,
When men lived blithely 'neath the sun,
Loving earth's beauty and its pleasure,
Rejoicing in abundant measure,
Nor deeming joy and sin were one.
Such the Renaissance.   Those you name,
Save only Raphæl are in soul
Still of the Middle Age; the same
Blind piety, although control
Of skill artistic they've acquired
In some degree; they remnants are

Of darker ages, and they jar
Upon the gay Renaissance life.
By other dreams they are inspired,
And with its spirit are at strife.
The things that Italy contains
Most worthy of our care and pains
Are works in which the human form
Stands forth before us fresh and warm,
Painted by Titian or Veronese,
Tintoret or Palma Vecchio,
Or other master hands; yes, these,
And those bright relics of the time
Of Grecian life which clearly show
How fair her art and how sublime.

FELIX.

Too much the outward you esteem,
The truer life is that within;
And in those upturned faces beam
Pure gentle souls that know not sin.
As to the soul the body yields
In dignity, so he who paints
The souls of sinners or of saints,
Yea, of the woodlands and the fields,
Is the true artist, and not he
Who reproduces faithfully
The outward form, but can not give
Our souls, which only truly live.

ANTONIO.

Oh Felix, we can ne'er agree
On art.   Perhaps the fault's with me.
I love fair, rounded, plastic shapes,
The subtile soul from me escapes.
I love this world too much to yearn
For saintly dreams to which you turn.
With Epicurus the divine
I am content when bright eyes shine,
And snowy arms about me twine.
      And now, Sebastian, let me say
The Lady Lalage to-night
Receives her friends, and bids me pray
Her invitation you'll not slight.
You now have mourned beyond a year,
And in the world should re-appear.

FELIX.

'Twere best to go.   In solitude
At first our forces are renewed;
But if too long we dwell alone
Morbid we grow and inward brood
Until the spirit's health is gone.

SEBASTIAN.

The Lady Lalage,— I recall
That once I met her at a ball,
A lady handsome, rather tall,

With rounded and voluptuous form
And great black eyes and raven hair,
A woman dazzling, strangely fair.
But yesternight however warm
The invitation, I'd declined;
But now quite different is my mind.
I am all weary of these books,
And fain would see how woman looks.
I gladly will attend you there.

SCENE IV.

A Street.   Sebastian and Antonio leaving
Lalage's House.

NIGHT.

SEBASTIAN.

The Lady Lalage is strangely fair.

ANTONIO.

Be not entangled in the snare
Of that most wondrous raven hair.
Many have languished in their pain,
Adoring her, but all in vain.
She seemeth proof against their arts,
And coldly smiles at breaking hearts.
You'll idly seek from virtue's ways
Her to seduce — She never strays.

SEBASTIAN.

Much you mistake.   I do not nurture
The least design against her virtue.
I would not, friend, to save my life
Seek to mislead our host's fair wife.

ANTONIO.

All that does very well to say.
I have known others talk that way
Who yet have ended otherwise.
There is a charm in woman's eyes
That plays sad havoc with our morals
When cheeks are pink and lips are corals.

SEBASTIAN.

I fear your long sojourn in France
Has robbed you of your little chance
To be a saint.

ANTONIO.

        I sometimes think
The Frenchman's views of life correct.
We have in youth a brief romance,
Then marry, settle down and sink
Into the humdrum commonplace,
Nor further joys of love expect.
Far different with the Gallic race.
Long as they live the dulcet game
Of love they play with subtle art,

And age itself can scarcely tame
The fire that burns their amorous heart.
'Tis most immoral, you will say,
But when they all are in the play
None can complain, and surely life
Is sweetened by the tender strife.
Nor is it wise to be too strict.
The world forgives with ready ease
A sinner's sin —'tis what's expected;
But when the virtuous are detected
At fault, men buzz like angry bees,
Rejoiced their venom to inflict.

SEBASTIAN.

You say that many men have courted
Fair Lalage?

ANTONIO.

        So 'tis reported;
You know that I have absent been.
And truly 'tis no heinous sin
To love a woman fair as she.

SEBASTIAN.

And all you say have loved in vain?

ANTONIO.

She has been heedless of their pain,
So all aver the fact to be.
And yet I own it seems to me

She should not be beyond all reach;
She seems from Lilith to descend.

SEBASTIAN.

What would you say, my worthy friend?

ANTONIO.

You know that Adam, as they teach,
Possessed an earlier wife than Eve.
We thus two female types receive,
Both needful for man's happiness.
Eve's daughter with her chaste caress
Consoles us in our heart's distress,
And doth our home with children bless.
The other lures to love's delights,
To lawless passion, sleepless nights,
To kisses fierce that burn the soul,
To joys that brook no law's control,
And with her passionate seduction
Allures us oft to our destruction,
But also brings a bliss intense
So keen 'tis worth the consequence.
Man needs them both, and incomplete
His life unless he both has tried,
One born to be a blushing bride,
For lawless joys the other meet.
Sometimes it happens, sad to say,
Eve's gentle daughters tread the way
Of Lilith's children.   All unfit,

With faltering steps they follow it,
Their souls revolting 'gainst their shame,
And grieving for their sullied fame.
And sometimes Lilith's daughters take
The place of Eve's, and so become
Mothers and wives, but most succumb
To their own instincts, forced to slake
Their burning thirst for wanton joy.
Not well our Lilith's we employ.
The Greeks much better comprehend
Their value.   Helen was decended
From Lilith; so the lovely Thaïs,
Phryne, Aspasia, charming Laïs.
They were adored in that bright era
By all who worshiped at the shrine
Of Aphrodite the divine.
Beside the wife stood the hetæra,
Both honored in their separate spheres;
The one the angel of the home
Whose chaste affections did not roam,
The other tending on the fires
Of Aphrodite Pandemos,
Goddess of uncontrolled desires,
With her wild infant Himeros,
Who hovering by her side appears.
Possessed of both, man was content,
His every wish was satisfied;
But now all honor is denied

To those of Lilith's fair descent
Unless they imitate the carriage
Of Eve's chaste daughters, and consent
To wear the heavy chain of marriage.
So, many who were born to be
Hetæræ passionate and free
Bow all unsuited to the yoke
Till time and circumstance provoke
Them to rebellion.   Such to me
Appears the Lady Lalage.

SEBASTIAN.

No, No, my friend, 'tis plain you err,
And gross injustice do to her
In this opinion.   That she's pure
Although much courted, you assure.
A woman in her richest prime
Wedded to one bowed down by time,
Who yet maintains her fame untarnished
Is not a mere hetæra varnished.
Your types sometimes in one combined
Present to us the perfect woman,
With fascinations superhuman,
Ardent and passionate and kind,
Fitted for love's supreme delight,
Yet pure as in the silver light
Of chastest moons; and such to me
Appears the Lady Lalage.

ANTONIO.

You are, I see, caught in the snare
Of that luxuriant raven hair.
Do you suppose I did not see
Your doting o'er her bosom's charms,
The snowy neck, the tapered arms,
Her face that Helen's well might be?
All through the evening I observed
How humbly at her feet you served,
What burning glances you directed
On charms by finest lace protected.
Already I perceive you break
The tenth commandment for her sake.

SEBASTIAN.

I covet not my neighbor's wife.
Although her charms I may admire
Pure admiration they inspire,
Nor waken love's tumultuous strife.

ANTONIO.

'Tis well;· and yet I do not see
Why you should not accepted be.
You are of splendid family,
Of comely person, courteous manners,
And once fought well 'neath Cupid's banners;
And she, in rich maturity
Is of the age when women are

Most worthy to be wooed and won.
Sweeter than girlish love by far,
Sweetest of all beneath the sun,
Is that of woman in her prime,
When full development the mind
And body have alike attained.
Then she is best, then is the time
To win her love.   Then she is kind
And strong and passionate and sweet;
Then is her witchery complete.
The Lady Lalage has gained
That happy age, and if you win
Her love, the joy were worth the sin.

SEBASTIAN.

Then why not claim her for your own?

ANTONIO.

Because 'twere vain; but she has shown
To you more favors than to all
Who yet have bowed beneath her thrall.
Besides, she is too much for me.
An Epicurean, I sip
The wine of love with sapient lip,
And wish no Phædra such as she.
I but aspire to facile loves,
To women soft as cooing doves;
I wish alone love's wanton joy,
And not fierce passions that destroy.

Barbarians when they seize on wine
Swill it as greedily as swine
Until, like brutes, all overcome
They lie stretched out inert and dumb;
While men of culture fill the glasses,
Inhale its perfume, sip it slowly,
Appreciate its flavor wholly,
And taste each rudy drop that passes,
Seeking alone exhiliration,
Nor yielding to intoxication.
So 'tis with love; the prudent man
Pursues it as a pleasing game,   .
Draws from it all the joy he can,
But flies its desolating flame.
The kind of love that bringeth pleasure
Is love in just sufficient measure
To wake desire, not love that burns,
And which too oft to anguish turns.
If I mistake not, Lalage
Has in her blood volcanic fire.
To tigress loves I don't aspire,
The frailer ones suffice for me

SEBASTIAN.

I care not for your light amours.
If I must love I want the the stress
Of real passion, and a bliss
So keen it borders on distress,

The burning joy of frenzied kiss,
The wildly passionate embrace
Of arms that cling and interlace;
'Tis love like that my soul allures.

ANTONIO.

'Tis plain you do not comprehend
The art of living pleasantly.
Instead of hurrying to the end
We long should linger by the way,
Enjoying love's delicious play.
As men become more civilized
Less is the mere possession prized,
And more the pleasure of pursuit.
The man who fishes with a net
Knows nothing of the joy of angling.
More quickly he the fish may get,
Them basely in the mesh entangling;
But that is worthy of a brute.
Not so the cultured angler fishes;
A fragile reed alone he wishes;
With this he hooks the largest trout,
And plays him with infinite skill,
Letting him first dart all about,
Now here, now there, just as he will,
Forcing the hook deep in his gill,
Until his strength is wearied out;
And when at length the sport is o'er

He pulls him gently to the shore.
The art of love is just the same,
'Tis thus the artist plays the game.

SEBASTIAN.

I must confess I have no wish
The ladies to confound with fish.
If I should love 'twould be sincere,
And would not end with mere possession.
'Twould be inflamed by each concession,
And would increase from year to year.
'Tis therefore not worth while to waste
Such sage advice on me, I fear.

ANTONIO.

You have one virtue very great
In one who would o'ercome the fair.
Smoking has kept more women chaste
Than virtue has, beyond compare.
When ready to capitulate
And give the kiss whence follows all,
How oft their nostrils are offended,
The spell is broken, all is ended,
And he knows not what caused his fall.

SEBASTIAN.

Again you do exaggerate.
True love resideth in the soul,
Nor on tobacco hangs its fate.

ANTONIO.

It is the senses that control.
If not, why don't you love profess
For one that's ugly, old and wrinkled,
Whose scanty locks with gray are sprinkled,
But who all virtues doth possess?
A man's a pig in gilded sty,
And she who understands the art
To rouse and then to satisfy
His appetite will rule his heart.
The chaste, cold wife oft wanders why
She is forsook for one less fair,
Nor comprehends she should employ
Her luscious charms for amorous joy
To bind him firmly in love's snare.
The women who have conquered men,
And ruled as tyrants o'er their hearts,
The Circes who by magic arts
Have changed them back to beasts again,
The Cleopatras for whose smiles
Kingdoms are lost without regret,
Are those who by seductive wiles
Men's appetites for pleasure whet
Until, all frenzied by desire,
They burn with a consuming fire.
And there are those whose kiss has power
To sear the soul as with a flame,
Making it blind to every aim

Save passion from that fatal hour.
'Twas such that lured the angels down
From heaven to dwell upon the earth,
Forgetting their celestial birth
And casting off their starry crown.
Love is a hunger for the charms
Of handsome face and dimpled arms,
Of bosom round and firm and white,
Of all that tempts to love's delight.
'Tis in excitement of the senses
Most frequently that it commences.
It is a singular compound
Of friendship and of sensual passion
Blended together in such fashion
That hard it is to trace the bound.

SEBASTIAN.

You are not half correct, my friend.
Love is a true affinity
Between two souls that strongly tend
To join together and to blend
In sweet and perfect unity.
Love is the purest, noblest feeling
That man can know.   It lift us up,
Sweetening the contents of life's cup,
The joys of paradise revealing.
Do not endeavor to degrade
The purest thing that God has made.
Nature createth nothing single,

But every thing has each its mate,
Toward which its longings gravitate,
With which it yearns to meet and mingle.
Nothing is in itself complete;
All yearns to find its counterpart.
When loving heart is joined to heart,
Then 'tis we live, then life is sweet.
True bliss is only found in love;
And much I think the Christians err
Forbidding marriage ties with her
Without whose presence heaven above
Would loose its charm.   For womanhood
The heart of man must ever yearn;
And God declared it was not good
Man should alone on earth sojourn,
And for his wife created Eve.
Man's love for woman is so strong
That I confess I can't conceive
A heaven where marriage don't belong.
I do not wish the Moslem heaven
With seventy black-eyed houris given.
I long for love, love sweet and pure,
'Tis that that doth my soul allure.
What you call love is but caprice.
Mere sensual joy you long to taste,
And move toward that with brutal haste,
And when 'tis won, all longings cease.
True love is humble, worshiping

Its object as a sacred thing.
The lover scarce dares lift his eyes
To her, an angel from the skies.
A look, a pressure of the hand,
Fills him with transport, and he thinks
That in a smile heaven's joy he drinks.
Upon a height she seems to stand,
Where he can never hope to reach.
He worships humbly from afar
Until at length he dares beseech
Her love, as one might pray a star.
You look on woman as the spider
Looks on the fly it seeks to capture.
You'd first degrade and then deride her.
Nothing you know of love's true rapture.

ANTONIO.

Love is the war between the sexes.
'Tis woman's to resist aggression
Until at length she comes to fall,
And then to bind him 'neath her thrall.
Men's part is to attain possession,
And yet to keep his freedom all.

SEBASTIAN.

You cynicism somewhat perplexes.
But well you know that love is not
A state of war, but one of peace,
The sweetest known to mortal lot.

Love you confound with mere caprice
But let this cynic mocking cease.
And now that we have reached your gate,
Good night, my friend, 'tis very late.

ANTONIO.

Good night, Sebastian; through your sleep
Seductive dreams of her will creep.
And friend, to-morrow you'll go see
The charming Lady Lalage.

SCENE V.

Felix and Sebastian.

FELIX.

My dear Sebastian, I must beg of you
No longer our departure to delay.
Great danger threatens should we longer stay.
Without solicitude I can not view
Your growing love for Lady Lalage.

SEBASTIAN.

'Twere needless to deny I feel the charm
Of her great beauty, but for your alarm
There is no just occasion that I see.

FELIX.

You love her more, Sebastian, than you own;
Else long ago to Italy we'd flown.

SEBASTIAN.

I must admit that her society
I find most pleasing.   She is passing fair,
And with her charm and grace can none compare.

FELIX.

Sebastian, I beseech you to beware.
Think who she is — she is another's wife.
Through degradation and through shame alone
Can you e'er hope to claim her as your own.
Would you polute her bright and spotless life?

SEBASTIAN.

Not for the world.

FELIX.

            Then come away with me.
In such a case the brave are those who flee.
Be not too confident.   Love is a power
That creeps upon us in the unguarded hour.
At first we smile such puny chains to see,
And let him wind them round us as he will,
Nor fearing aught of such weak bonds until
It is too late, and then we strive in vain
To break his slender, adamantine chain.
You can to-day part from her, but to-morrow
May be too late, and endless shame and sorrow,
Yea, death itself, may punish your delay.

SEBASTIAN.

Felix, there is no cause for this dismay.
The Lady Lalage is far above
The thought of yielding to a guilty love;
And you should know that I shall ne'er offend
Against the rules of honor, my good friend.

FELIX.

Trust not too much to honor.   When the fire
Of passion burns, when love and hot desire
Seethe in the bosom, honor's voice, unheard,
Serves only to reproach us when we've erred
Beyond redemption.   Love's a malady
That prays upon the soul insidiously.
It creeps upon us as a pleasing langour,
And we are lost ere danger we suspect.
The Greeks were wise who saw it in the anger
Of Gods who men on seas of passion wrecked,
To punish their offending.

SEBASTIAN.

If 'tis sent
By wrathful gods on men as punishment,
The deities must bear the blame of sin.
So thought the Greeks, nor Helen did destoy,
But gladly brought her back from burning Troy,
And Menelaus led her proudly in
To reign again as queen in Sparta's halls.

FELIX.

But we know better.   Love legitimate
Is pure and chaste, nor comes it from the hate
Of envious gods, and when its chain enthralls,
Leading us on through flowery paths to where
Stands Hymen's alter, we may follow on
Rejoicing, by the tender impulse drawn.
But when we find another's wife too fair,
We know at once the guilt of our desire,
And sternly should repress the nascent fire.

SEBASTIAN.

And yet for both the passion is the same,
Though one meets your approval, one your blame.
Love is a passion planted in the breast
By heaven to make man's earthly sojourn blest.
Gentle and sweet the thoughts that it instills,
Binding two hearts together till each thrills
In unison of bliss.   When two souls meet
Born to be mates, instinctivly they greet
Each other — love awakes by God's decree.
And yet you say that when some man has given
A woman to another, she must be
Forever his, and from her true love flee,
Thus placing man's decrees above the laws of heaven.

FELIX.

'Tis not Sabastian's soul that speaketh thus,
But that wild passion that o'ermasters it.

None better knows that human edicts writ
'Gainst such amours but serve to ratify
The laws which God himself ordained for us.
And dread the consequence if you defy
God's laws and man's. I do not speak of you,
For you I know impervious are to fear;
But think of her to whom you fondly sue,
Whom you would die for, rather than a tear
Should dim the melting lustre of her eye.
If she should fall, all hope of joy were gone.
She never could be happy with the sense
Of guilt upon her soul. You'd lead her on
To secret sin, but public shame would follow;
Her ruin and your own the consequence.
So do not yield to reasoning so hollow.

SEBASTIAN.

Felix, you're right, but, pray you, do not think
That ever I have thought of loving her
Save with a chaste affection that would shrink
From the bare thought of leading her to err.
And if I were inclined, she has not shown
The slightest sign that could encourage me
To venture aught against a purity
Spotless as snow by mountain breezes blown.
This eve, however, I will bid adieu,
And then to-morrow I'll away with you.

FELIX.

'Twere better if your farewell you would send
By letter as we started.

SEBASTIAN.

                    No, my friend,
'Twere most discourteous.   I will go and say
Farewell, and then to Italy away.

SCENE VI.

Sebastian and Lalage in gardens of Lalage's house.

NIGHT.

SEBASTIAN.

Thou art so beautiful, temptingly beautiful,
    Kiss me once, kiss me once ere I depart,
Long have I waited, love, humble and dutiful,
    Hiding the passion consuming my heart.

Deep in the breast of the mountain is burning
    Fire that is hidden there far from our sight,
Seething and surging with passionate yearning,
    Striving to issue forth into the light.

Long by the strength of the mountain subjected,
    Writhing and twisting, it struggles in vain;
Fiercer the strength that it yet has collected,
    Bursting at length like a wolf from its chain.

So from its fetters my passion has broken,
  Bearing me on to distruction and sin;
Words I should perish before they were spoken
  Rush to my lips, and will not be held in.

Lead us, oh, lead us not into temptation,
  Such is the prayer that alone is worth all.
Cruel was He that at Eden's creation
  Planted the Knowledge Tree causing the fall.

Ever unconsciously, sweet, thou has tempted me,
  Tempted me past my endurance to bear;
God from man's weakness has never exempted me,
  And thou wert ever too temptingly fair.

Thou art so beautiful, temptingly beautiful,
  I can no longer my passion control,
I can no longer be humble and dutiful,
  Kiss me but once though the price be my soul.

LALAGE.

Sebastian, Sebastian, be silent I pray,
Oh, seek not, oh, seek not to lead me astray.
If truly thou lovest, thou wishest me pure,
Then into temptation, oh, do not allure.

SEBASTIAN.

Ah! half thou confessest my love is returned;
The fire that so long in my bosom has burned

Hath wakened an answering flame in thy heart,
Oh, kiss me then, kiss me then ere I depart.

LALAGE.

Sebastian, Sebastian, 'twere vain to deny
That often in secret I've stifled a sigh.
I own that I love thee, but oh, I implore,
Accept this confession, demanding no more.

SEBASTIAN. (*Seizing her in his arms.*)

Oh, speak to the river that rolls to the sea,
To the lion that wooeth his terrible mate,
To the hurricane driving the ship to its fate,
And bid them be quiet, but speak not to me.
Thou lovest me, lovest me, then thou art mine,
And nothing shall part us as long as life lasts,
And when at the day of the judgment divine
The earth from her bosom her children outcasts,
Around thee mine arms I shall lovingly twine,
And smile at the blare of the trumpeter's blasts.

LALAGE. (*Disengaging herself.*)

'Tis thou who has wished it, but dost thou conceive
The force of the passion that thou dost invoke?
As long as life lasts unto thee I shall cleave;
I am thine, thou art mine, till the day when the stroke
Of the scythe of the reaper shall part us in twain.
In my breast evermore thou as master shalt reign;

When thou ceasest to love me, Sebastian, I die —
From the depths of my bosom thou hearest my cry.

· *(She throws herself into his arms.)*

SABASTIAN.

Oh, speak not of ceasing to love thee, my sweet;
Till the borders of time and eternity meet
I am thine, my belovèd, and even in death
I shall murmer thy name with my last fleeting breath.

(He kisses her.)

How sweet, oh how sweet is a kiss from thy lips!
The bee that on Hybla the honey-dew sips
Knows nothing of sweetness, knows nothing of bliss,
They only are found in thy ravishing kiss.

(He kisses her again.)

LALAGE.

Oh, do not despise me because I thus yield.
Against thee my bosom I could not have steeled.
I have loved thee in silence since first thou wert known.
Deal gently with one so completely thine own.

SEBASTIAN.

Despise thee, my darling! I worship the spot
That is touched by thy feet, and I envy the lot
Of the grass that is pressed by thy delicate tread.
Speak not of despising, I worship instead.
The evening when first to thy mansion I came

There awoke in my bosom a passionate flame
Which shall burn ever brighter as time shall roll on,
And reign in my breast at eternity's dawn.
Couldst thou teach me to love the Creator on high
With a love as devout as the passionate sigh
That I breathe at thy feet, then a saint I should be
Like the saints that once wandered by blue Gallilee.

LALAGE.

Then wilt thou forsake me, oh, wilt thou depart?
Oh, now it is thine wilt thou shatter my heart?
I know that the land where thou goest is fair
With a beauty denied to the land of thy birth,
That the blossoming oranges perfume the air,
And the songs of the angels are heard on the earth.
I know that our palaces are but as sties
Compared with its mansions of marble and gold,
Where the glitter of jewels doth dazzle the eyes
And the glories of art as the sands are untold.
I know that its women have charms never given
To those that are born in our homelier clime,
Recalling the peris that wandered from heaven
To mingle with men in the world's lusty prime.
But a heart that will love with devotion as true
As the one that now burns in my passionate breast
In vain wilt thou seek 'neath that firmament blue,
In those mansions that seem the abodes of the blest.

SEBASTIAN.

From the peaks of the Alps to Calabria's cape,
From the temples of Rome to the blue Appenine,
There is nought that in beauty can distantly ape
The least of thy charms, oh, my angel divine.

LALAGE.

And yet thou wilt leave me and wander afar
To the land where the olive and vine interlace,
Where soon thou wilt worship a lovelier star,
Forgetting my grief for a handsomer face.

SEBASTIAN.

Should Venus in person descend from above
In all of her beauty, imploring my love,
I should tell her a goddess still fairer than she
Had promised the queen of my bosom to be.

LALAGE.

And yet wilt thou leave me, and, wandering forth,
Wilt seek the delights of that beautiful clime;
While I pine for thy love in the gloom of the north,
In that land of the sun thou wilt reck not the time.

SEBASTIAN.

If the wealth of the Indies were offered to me
With all of the gems in the caves of the sea,
If the crown of the Cæsars my guerdon should be,
I would not one moment be parted from thee.

LALAGE.

Oh, blest be the lips which that promise have spoken!
It has flooded my bosom with raptuous bliss.
I know that thy pledges will never be broken,
And I seal thee as mine with this passionate kiss.

(*Kisses him passionately.   Then starts back.*)

But what wilt thou think of a woman who thus
Surrenders herself when thy love is scarce told?
Such frankness in passion becometh not us,
Who to lovers' appeals should be modestly cold.

SEBASTIAN. (*Clasping her in his arms.*)

Oh, speak not of modesty; that but begins
Where love terminates, and the lover who wins
The heart of his mistress finds nothing of that
In the path to the goal of his hopes to combat.
But hark, they are seeking thee, we must return,
And I must surrender thee back to the crowd.
Oh, kiss me again, yet again.   How I yearn
To hold thee as mine with a passion avowed.

LALAGE.

Oh, scarcely I've found thee! So soon must we part?
Then press me again, yet again to thy heart,
And know that though absent I seemingly be,
My spirit forever shall hover by thee.

SEBASTIAN.

Another — another — a last parting kiss!
Ah, almost I swoon with excess of my bliss.
But now my belov'd, I must bid thee farewell
Though the word in my bosom doth sound as a knell.
Then adieu to thee, darling, adieu to thee, sweet.

LALAGE.

Farewell, my Sebastian, till soon we shall meet.

SCENE VII.

Lalage alone in her chamber.

NIGHT.

LALAGE.

Sebastian comes to-night, yet I am sad.
I wonder to what end this love will lead?
I care not if it ever be with him,
Feasting upon the kisses of his mouth
As on the nectar of the blessed gods.
I fear 'twill be my ruin, but if I
Can sweep through Hades locked in his embrace,
Even as Francesca in old Dante's song,
My fate will be most happy.   Oh, the love
I bear him! Naught I knew of happiness
Till pressed against his heart! 'Tis half an hour
Before he comes. My harp is here, I'll sing an ancient
    song
To cheat the lagging moments while I wait.

SINGS.

I sailed upon a river,
  It sparkled in the light,
Its crystal waters rippled
  With laughter pure and bright.

I drifted down the river,
  And still it smiled to me,
And sweeter grew its beauty
  As it bore me toward the sea.

And I had no thought of danger
  As I watched the lovely stream .
On which the sun was resting
  With fond caressing beam.

I saw the current quicken,
  But I would not seek the shore;
The river was so charming
  That I loved it more and more,

And ever swifter flowed it,
  But still I looked and smiled,
For I loved that beauteous river
  Whose charms my soul beguiled.

And now I hear the cataract
   That plunges into gloom;
'Tis now too late to struggle,
   I can not 'scape my doom.

Oh, river, I have loved thee
   With a passion deep and strong,
With a love that perhaps was guilty,
   But it seemed too sweet for wrong.

And now thou bearest me onward
   To the dark and cruel grave,
And still I love so madly
   My life I would not save.

Upon thy breast I am happy,
   Though thou whilrest me down to the tomb,
And gazing upon thy bosom
   I smilingly meet my doom.

Now louder grows the tumult,
   I near the awful brink;
Oh, kiss me lovely river.
   Oh, kiss me ere I sink.

'Tis a sad old song, and makes me sadder still.
I wonder why Sebastian loves it so?
Would he were here.   My heart is sore oppressed,
And I'm afraid.   A chill creeps over me.

I wish that rat would stop his knawing there,
It grates upon my nerves; and how the owls
Are hooting in the fir trees! Now one laughs,
A cruel laugh that makes my blood run cold.
How weak I am, I who was once so brave.
The faintest sound of the uncanny night
Doth make me start.   And now that cat!
There's something strangely human in their cry
Like the long wail of souls in agony.
Was that a footstep yonder in the hall?
No, 'twas the wind, and yet I tremble so!

(*Polycarp rushes in.*)

POLYCARP.

Thou cursed harlot, thou dost wait for him!
Die, die!   (*Stabs her.*)

LALAGE.

Oh, murder! thou hast killed me! Oh,
                Sebastian!   (*Dies.*)

(*A long pause.   Polycarp stands looking at
the body.   At last Sebastian enters by the window.*)

SEBASTIAN.

Oh, God! oh, God!

POLYCARP. (*insane.*)

Ha, Ha, come in and share the wedding feast!
Come, come, and dance, it is a joyous night!

Ha, come and dance, young master, come and dance!
Dost not thou not hear the fiddles and the harp?
Come in, and we will sup right merrily.
Come in, come in!   They say that I am old,
But I will show them that I still am young.
Ha, thou shalt see me dancing with the bride.
Ha ha, they say she married me to save
Her father from distruction.   Foolish tongues!
Thou soon shalt witness how she dotes on me.
Is she not lovely?   Look, the coral there
Upon her bosom.   Some fools call it blood,
But it is coral, coral for the bride.
Come dance, my friend, come dance, and we will drain
A bumper to her health.   Is she not fair?
And she will soon be mine, yea, mine, mine, mine!
Ha ha, I laugh at those sleek young gallants
Who pine away for hunger of her charms.
Ha ha, come, come, we will away to revel!

SEBASTIAN.

Oh, my God, my God!

(Sinks swooning on the body.)

SCENE VIII.

Sebastian and Felix crossing the Alps dressed as wandering scholars with scrip and staff.

SEBASTIAN.

Look at the storm fiends
Yonder below us
Mustering their legions
O'er the abyss.

See their black pinions
Beating together,
Hear how they mutter,
Hear how they hiss.

FELIX.

Fiercely the tempest
Rages below us,
But up above us
Bright is the sky.

Glorious, majestic
Round us the mountains
Lift their white summits
Gleaming on high.

SEBASTIAN.

See how the demons
Gather together
Forming their phalanx
For the assault.

Demons of darkness
Crowding in legions
Ready to escalade
Heaven's blue vault.

FELIX.

Gaze not thus fixedly
Into the chasm
Lest, growing dizzy,
Downward thou fall.

SEBASTIAN.

Hark how they mutter!
Now they behold me
See how they beckon!
On me they call!

FELIX.

Bend thy glance upward
Into the heavens,
Dread the abyss'
Desperate charm.

Strange how the perilous
Depths will attract us,
Luring us wonderfully
Down to our harm.

Stars in the firmament,
Weary of shining,
Dash themselves franticly
Down from their height.

Women of purity
Spotless as angels,
Lured by the precipice,
Plunge into night.

Look not thus fixedly
Into the chasm,
Tread not thus recklessly
Close to its brink.

SEBASTIAN.
See they are rising
Rapidly toward us!
Some through the fir trees
Cautiously slink,

Others more boldly
Straight through the ether
On their broad pinions
Toward us advance.

Hark to the tumult!
Each one is mounting,
Shaking his terrible
Far-flashing lance.

FELIX.

Swiftly the tempest
Upward is rolling.
Seek we a shelter
Under this rock.

SEBASTIAN.

Hark to the horrible
Roar of the storm-fiends!
Even the mountains
Quake at the shock.

FELIX.

Upward the hurricane
Toward us is rushing;
Plant thy feet firmly,
Cling with thy hands.

SEBASTIAN.

See how the storm-fiends
Splinter the fir trees;
Nothing their passionate
Fury withstands.

Look, they are mounting,
Countless in numbers,
Coming to dash us
Down to the grave.

Still they are mounting,
Greater their fury,
Hear how they mutter,
Hear how they rave.

FELIX.

Great is the danger!
Seize this projection
Of the firm adamant!
Desperately cling!

SEBASTIAN,

Bounding so frightfully
Through the scared ether,
Ever advancing,
Upward they spring.

FELIX

Steady! it reaches us;
O'er us it surges.
Now up above us
Passeth the storm.

SEBASTIAN.

Look at the storm-fiends!
Where are they bearing
On their black pinions
Lalage's form?

See her long tresses
Tossed by the whirlwind,
See how they flutter,
See how they flow!

Loose me! I'll follow
Upward to heaven,
Or to hell's caverns
Yawning below.

Loose me, I tell thee.
See, she is weeping,
See, she is stretching
Toward me her arms!

FELIX.

Ne'er will I loose thee!
'Tis but a phantom,
Born of thy passionate
Sorrow, that charms.

SEBASTIAN.

Loose me, I tell thee,
See how she beckons!

Oh, they are bearing her
Far from my sight!

FELIX.

Thou art distracted.
Ne'er will I suffer thee
Deathward to dash thyself
Down from this height.

SEBASTIAN.

Loose me, I beg of you!
See, they are bearing her
Over the mountains
Swiftly away!

See she is beckoning!
Quick must I fly to her.
Oh, I am dizzy!
Loose me, I pray.

(*Sinks fainting upon the ground.*)

SCENE IX.

Sebastian and Felix among the Appenines.

FELIX.

See the wondrous beauty of this region,
Bathed in radiance by the rising sun,
See the gilded mists below us mounting
Like blest souls whose work of love in done.

Rising from the plains outstretched beneath us
Where the vineyards alternate with fields,
And where Nature with unfailing kindness
Hundredfold the bounteous harvest yields.

See, above, the awful mountain standing,
Lifting in the blue its silver crest,
While below, it folds the storm cloud proudly
As a sable mantle round its breast.

Here 'mid nature's beauty and her grandeur
Man's vexed soul may find an hour of peace
As a weary child upon the bosom
Of its mother feels its troubles cease.

SEBASTIAN.
Nature is a stepdame to her children,
Not a mother tender, kind and true.
What cares she although we all should perish,
What cares she how black our sorrow's hue?

Even when she smiles in sweetest beauty
Death she sows with a remorseless hand.
Yonder lovely mist that toward us rises
Hath left fever stalking through the land.

Not a gentle mother who protects us,
Not a just one punishing the wrong;
Guilt and innocence alike are stricken
As she drives her blood-stained car along.

From the mighty monsters that have vanished
To the weaklings of the present hour
Nature doth create but for destruction,
Bearing children only to devour.

Call not her a mother who afflicts us
Needlessly with sorrow and with pain,
Who, all careless of our guilt or virtue,
Deals to us our happiness or bane.

FELIX.

Great the mystery of earth's creation,
And 'tis not for us poor creeping things
To pass judgment on the power almighty
At whose beck the universe upsprings.

Yonder sun that in his glory rises,
Bearing light and joy to wakening earth,
To a power beneficent as mighty
Owes the awful splendor of his birth.

Canst thou doubt the firmament above us
With its countless multitude of stars
Sweeping each in its predestined orbit,
Ruled by laws which discord never mars,

Was by God for noble ends created?
Why call forth this wondrous whole from naught?
If it be not for a worthy purpose
God had not so great a marvel wrought.

We are but an atom of the Cosmos,
Nor can comprehend the mighty whole,
Feeble ants in darkness ever crawling,
While above our heads the planets roll.

SEBASTIAN.

Vast the Cosmos, and we judge it only
By the fragment to our sight revealed,
And we find it cruel, cold, remorseless,
To man's cry for mercy ever steeled.

FELIX.

Man offending 'gainst the laws of Nature
Bears the punishment of his offence,
But on those her righteous laws obeying
She bestows a bounteous recompense.

SEBASTIAN.

Nature hath her laws, but all their bounty
To the cunning or the strong is paid,
And to her the innocent and gentle
Call in vain for mercy or for aid.

FELIX.

Without struggle there is no improving,
Life's a conflict, but it is the best,
Yea, the noblest, strongest and most worthy
Who emerge with victory's wreath possessed.

SEBASTIAN.

So Achilles and great Hector perished
On the vulture-haunted plains of Troy,
While the coward rabble homeward sailing
Greeted wives and native land with joy.

Those surviving in life's bitter struggle
Are the ones best fitted to survive
In a world where fraud and force still triumph,
Where the wicked as the bay tree thrive.

FELIX.

Not the wicked but the wise and prudent
Are the victors in the war of life.
Thus doth Nature teach to man her wisdom,
Forcing him to gird him for the strife.

SEBASTIAN.

Nature careth naught for guilt or virtue,
But the rain doth fall on both alike,
And the wicked, by no scruples hampered,
May the blow with greater freedom strike.

FELIX.

Oft it doth appear the wicked triumph,
Justice overtakes them yet at last.
Just is Nature, and her vengeance cometh
Surest when we think the danger past.

SEBASTIAN.

Oftener is innocence afflicted
Than is guilt, for Nature careth not.
Man must rise above her to be noble,
Man must better be than is his lot.

Cruel she, therefore he must show mercy,
Careless she, therefore he must be just;
He must ever seek to make her better,
Struggle with her evil powers he must.

War against the Cosmos is man's duty,
Planting wheat where Nature soweth tares,
Striving ever to be good and noble,
Though of virtue's triumph he despairs.

No, my Felix, speak not thus in folly
Nature knoweth neither good nor ill,
Nor can give instruction in our duty
Right to follow with unflinching will.

FELIX.

Yet must thou confess in times of sorrow
On the breast of Nature peace is found,
Which we vainly seek in crowded cities
Where the tumults of man's life resound.

In her placid hours there is a calmness
Bringing peace to the afflicted soul,
In her wrath her trouble is so mighty
We forget our petty human dole.

Who can look on yonder verdant meadows
Where the mild-eyed oxen freely browse,
Or in pairs beneath the yoke subjected
Draw with patient tread the fruitful plows;

Who can look on yonder mountain summit,
Calm, majestic in its robe of snow,
Nor perceive the balm which Nature only
Can upon the bleeding heart bestow?

Nature is the one supreme consoler;
Unto her we fly when grief-oppressed,
And upon our wounds she spreadeth ointment,
Lulling sorrow with her songs to rest.

SEBASTIAN.

True it is that Nature bringeth calmness
To the soul tossed on the sea of life,
Weary of its never ending surging,
Weary of its tumult and its strife.

Then we fly from man's vexed petty passions
To the far-off mountain's gloomy pride,
To the vale where brooklets softly purling
Lure us on to linger by their side.

There the fever of our life forsakes us,
Peace descends into the troubled breast,
Lost is every sound of life's commotion,
And we find the sacred boon of rest.

So it was in former days, good Felix,
And when weary of the life of men
I would wander forth among the mountains,
By the babbling brook or reedy fen;

Sweet repose for weary brain and spirit
In the forest's silent depths I found,
And returned each time refreshed and strengthened,
As Antæus springing from the ground.

But the vulture now my heart is gnawing
As it gnawed the Titan on the peak,
And no more repose I find in Nature
Than Prometheus 'neath the vulture's beak.

FELIX.

Peace will yet come to thy troubled bosom,
Time alone can soften sorrow's sting.

SEBASTIAN.

No, I do not seek surcease of sorrow,
To my grief with all my soul I cling.

FELIX.

There are sorrows which we fondly cherish,
Yet in time they slowly slip away;
All in vain we press them to our bosom,
All in vain — we can not force their stay.

Every year the form beloved grows dimmer,
Seen through mists that rise before our gaze
And regretfully we look upon it,
Noting with remorse the gathering haze.

Sorrows come so bitter that it seemeth
We shall bear them with us to the tomb,
Yet with self-reproach we see them leaving
And our heart emerging from its gloom.

It is sad we would in vain be constant
To the grief so bitter and so dear;
But 'tis best the wound should not bleed always,
Nor should life be passed beside a bier.

'Tis not well the stricken soul should languish
Endlessly in unavailing pain,
Nor the past with its remorse should hold us,
Living duties should our thoughts enchain.

Who performs each day his daily duty,
Whether high or low his lot be cast,
Making earth the brighter for his presence,
Expiates the errors of his past.

See, Sebastian, see, the sun is mounting,
Let us mount with him to yonder height,
And behold the prospect vast and lovely
That will be unrolled before our sight.

SCENE X.

Sebastian and Felix.

SEBASTIAN.

Well, Felix, last night in the darkness reflecting,
I determined to leave for my far distant home.
Too long have I wandered, my duties neglecting,
From Venice to Naples, from Florence to Rome.
I have strolled by the shores of the blue Adriatic,
And have gazed o'er its glistening wavelets to where
Bright Venice appeared as a vision ecstatic,
A city suspended twixt ocean and air.
I have sailed in my gondola over its waters
Beneath pallid Luna's transfiguring light
Till the city seemed built by the sea for his daughters
Whose singing I heard in the hush of the night.
Sweet Naples, voluptuous queen of the South,
Who reclines in her beauty upon her green hills,
And smiles at Vesuvius' fiery mouth,
At the torrents of lava descending like rills;
And Milan's cathedral so wondrously wrought,

The dream of an artist embodied in stone,
So fair that it seems a creation of thought,
Nor built by the hands of mere mortals alone;
And Florence, proud monarch of Tuscany's land,
And Genoa seated o'er-looking the sea,
And Rome, ever first of the mighty and grand,
The ancient of days — have been traversed by me.
I have wandered through all with a heart heavy laden
With grief and remorse for the things of the past,
With a trouble which not all the pleasures of Aiden
Could make me forget ere the judgment day blast.
Yet much do I owe to this land of the sun,
But mostly, my noble friend Felix, to thee;
Ye have saved me from madness, whose work was
    begun,
And which would have left me a wreck on life's sea.
When first from that horrible trance I awoke,
Overwhelmed by my sorrow, my reason I cursed;
Oblivion in madness I fain would invoke,
Nor look on the woes of the future I durst.
But now I am calmer and stronger of soul,
And I thank thee, good Felix, for what thou hast done,
Though naught for the things of the past can console,
And the woof of my life all of black I have spun.
Most bitterly, friend, do I crave expiation
For the sins which so heavily weigh on my heart;
The joy of this land to my soul's desolation
A mockery seems, and for home I depart.

FELIX.

Thy purpose is noble and worthy, my friend,
But still with regret I should see thee set forth
Thus burdened with grief for the sorrowful north.
Through this land of the olive and vine let us wend
Our way for a while.   There are marvelous things
To whose recollection the memory clings,
There are wonders of beauty, of grandeur and gloom
That will haunt thee in dreams till thou sleepst in
    the tomb.
They wait for us yet in this land of the sun,
The search for whose charms we have scarcely begun.
Each hamlet secluded among the blue hills,
Where water is purling in crystaline rills,
Each village high-perched on the verdure-clad steep
Or gazing out over the amethyst deep,
Hath something of beauty delighting the eye,
Some belfry uplifting its form to the sky,
Some statue a world-famous sculptor hath wrought,
Some canvas where gloweth a heavenly thought,
A church where some vision of beauty is shrined,
And the worships of art and of God are combined.
And landscapes it offers as restful and fair
As those that were painted by Claude's magic hand,
Where the peace of the gods seem to gladden the land,
And the songs of the Muses to float on the air.
Oh, come my Sebastian, and let us explore
These regions so famous in classical lore.

From Como to ruined Tarentum we'll wander,
And over the wrecks of its greatness will ponder.
Campagna's green fields on which buffaloes browse
Where oppulent cities once stood in their pride;
Abbruzzi's wild paths where our footsteps arouse
The eagles that scream on the mountain's steep side;
The shore of the ocean, where Circe once dwelt,
And left to her daughters a part of her charms,
The full rounded bosom and tapering arms,
The witchery even Odysseus felt —
Through all we will stroll from the north to the south,
From the region of snow to the region of drouth,
Enjoying the marvels before us unrolled.
Then Sicily lures with her temples of old
The white of whose stones is now melted to gold,
With her delicate art which the Saracens taught,
And her plains where the Romans with Carthage once
     fought
For the world's domination, and Ætna's proud crest
Where we hear the fierce groans of the earth's tortured
     breast.
All beckon us onward. Come, friend, let us go,
This land on thy spirit its calm will bestow.
When its rest and its peace on thy soul have descended
Thou canst to the home of thy childhood return.

SEBASTIAN.

No, Felix, e'en here have my journeyings ended,
For the home of my fathers my bosom doth yearn.

No more in this land of all gladness I linger,
It suits not the gloom that envelopes my heart.
Last night as I slept, in a vision God's finger
Appeared, sternly pointing, and bade me depart.
I awoke and perceived that my soul's absolution
For the sins of the past I should never receive
Till I turned to my duty with fixed resolution
To lessen the number of mortals who grieve.
I would that the cross on my shoulder attaching
I might seek with Crusaders the Saracen shore,
My sword 'gainst the infidel's scimitar matching,
And expiate all in a torrent of gore.
I would that I might as an anchorite sainted
Go dwell in the desert in fasting and prayer,
Devoted to Him who with grief was acquainted,
And lashing my flesh in my frantic despair.
But harder the task that confronts us at present,
To live in the world and to act as we should,
Discharging our duties however unpleasant,
Determined toward all to be helpful and good.
So fearfully dashed on the reefs of life's ocean,
In the harbor of death I would moulder away,
No longer disturbed by its fevered commotion,
Untossed by its billows, undrenched by its spray.
But though for the peace of the grave I am yearning,
And gladly would lay me to sleep in the tomb,
Yet now to the land of my fathers returning,
My place in the world I shall sadly resume.

And there in the rigid performance of duty
I shall look for repose to my desolate heart,
Which vainly seeks comfort in Italy's beauty,
The blue of her skies and her marvels of art.

FELIX.

Then go, my Sebastian, I would not delay thee,
Thou hast found the true balm for the wound in thy
    breast.
For the good that thou doest may heaven repay thee
By filling thy soul with the peace of the blest.

SCENE XI.

*The Cathedral where Sebastian's Father and Lalage
are buried.*

Enter Sebastian.

SEBASTIAN. (*Approaching Lalage's grave.*)

I come, my love, in agony to lay
This wreath upon thy long neglected tomb.
Oh, why shouldst thou for my offending pay,
Thus stricken down in all thy beauty's bloom?
I would that I might lay me down instead
Where thou dost slumber there beneath the sod.
Why did I not precede thee to the dead,
And for my guilt to thee respond to God?

For love of me thou hast been doomed to death,
And I have seen it, yet I have not died.
I was not there to cheer thy dying breath,
Nor have I followed thee, my angel bride.
Thy soul, I know, doth wander through the blue,
Waiting for mine to join it in the sky:
In mine own blood this hand I would imbue
And fly to meet thy spirit there on high.
But, oh, I feel to thy celestial sphere
I can not mount with my sin-laden soul,
And that I must in anguish linger here
Till less unworthy of that heavenly goal.
Oh, sweetest Lalage thou wert my all,
My heaven on earth, my first, my only love.
And art thou gone forever?   Hear my call,
Have pity on my grief, though throned above.
In life thou wert the empress of my heart,
In death thou art the lodestar of my hope;
The bliss of paradise thou didst impart,
Its pearly gates thy soul to mine will ope.
Not that I merit there with thee to dwell,
But thou, I know, wilt intercede for me.
I could not drag thy spirit down to hell,
But thou, sweet love, canst draw me up to thee.
And thou wilt do it, for to mine thy soul
Is linked by an indissoluble bond,
Which hath united us in earthly dole,
And will unite us in the veiled beyond.

Thou wert by God to mortals lent awhile
To teach the beauty of the heavenly choir,
The sweet enchantment of the perfect smile,
The tender glance that sets the soul on fire.
To teach them how the heavenly throng excel
All found below in loveliness and worth,
To show them charms they could not else foretell,
And wean them from the baser things of earth.
Oh, Lalage, my bride, I bend me here
In agony of grief above thy grave,
Upon the marble shed the scalding tear,
And bowed by woe thy pardon humbly crave.

And now, my father, unto thee I turn,
And lay this wreath upon thy honored tomb.
Oh, father, how my tortured heart doth yearn
The old sweet converse with thee to resume.
Unworthy thy example was the life
I led in headstrong and unstable youth,
In careless revel or ignoble strife,
While scarcely heeded was thy lessons' truth.
But now, my father, doth my stricken soul
Recall with joy thy wisdom's sligthest word,
Which still avails to strengthen and console,
So priceless now, so little prized when heard.
The teachings that upon me then seemed lost
Now wake to life within my tortured breast;
Upon the sea of life by passion tossed,

I turn to thee for counsel and for rest.
Thou who in calmness and in wisdom soared
Above the frailties of my weaker heart,
Thy mighty mind with deepest knowledge stored,
A little of thy loftiness impart.
Teach me thy justice and thy self-control,
Thy resolution to be good and great,
Thy changeless magnanimity of soul,
Thy constancy beneath the blows of fate.
Teach me life's burden so to bear that when
Upon the further shore of time we meet,
Thou mayst not blush to look on me again,
But mayst a son not all unworthy greet.

Enter Priest.

PRIEST.

My son, I am rejoiced to see
Thou art returned, and most to find
That first thou hast betaken thee
To where God's worship is enshrined.
Rarely in times gone by didst thou
The knee in church or chapel bow,
And much it pleases me that now
To holier ways thou seemst inclined.

SEBASTIAN.

Returning from my long exile
I first have sought the blessèd dead,
Reposing 'neath this sacred pile,

The two bright stars whose life was shed
Upon my path — the one my sire,
Of whom I need not boast the worth,
And who hath trained me from my birth
In virtue's ways, though oft I've strayed,
And that sweet beam of heavenly fire,
That emanation from above
Who taught me all the bliss of love —
I've come to weep where they are laid.

PRIEST.

Thy filial piety, my son,
Deserves the highest praise, and I
Commend thy grief for loss of one
In worth so great, in blood so nigh.
But it afflicts me to perceive
That this unholy love of thine,
Like poison vipers, still doth twine
About thy soul.

SEBASTIAN.

             Thou needst not grieve.
That love in paradise was born,
And if in death all is not ended
(Though oft I doubt
If life is not a flame that death blows out,
A flickering spark
That gleams awhile, to vanish in the dark)

Then on the resurection morn
Her arms to me will be extended,
Striving to lift me up to where
In heaven she stands, supremely fair.

PRIEST.

Oh, speak not thus, full well thou knowest
How great the sin to lead astray
Another's wife.   The seed thou sowest,
In anguish wilt thou reap that day
Unless a true repentance win
Remission of thy grievous sin.

SEBASTIAN.

Is love a sin?   The holiest feeling
The heart of man can know, revealing
The joys of paradise above.
How is't a sin when God is love?

PRIEST.

My son, 'tis not such love as thine
That dwelleth in the breast divine.
Adulterate passion only draws
Man down to Hell's expanded jaws.
Open old Dante's book and read
Francesca's wail, and thence take heed.

SEBASTIAN.

Francesca is not Lalage.
My sainted Beatrice she'll be,

My grosser spirit upward lifting,
To where on clouds of purple drifting,
The heavenly chorus float and sing.
That Beatrice to whom we cling
As purity personified,
She was another's lawful bride.
All love is holy; great my guilt
In yielding to it if thou wilt,
But now by death 'tis sanctified,

PRIEST.

No, no, my son, thy guilty passion
Do not defend in guiltier fashion.
The urgent need dost thou not feel
To expiate the ruin brought
Upon her house, the havoc wrought
By thy mad folly?   Let us kneel
Here at God's altar and implore
Forgivness for thy sins of yore.

SEBASTIAN.

Most gladly, father, would I pray with thee,
Could I believe that God would answer me.
That child-like faith has vanished from my heart,
And Doubt sits there, nor will it thence depart.
Its sits enthroned within my troubled breast,
And rocketh to and fro, nor will it rest.
But bitterly, my father, do I yearn
For expiation — expiation stern;

I long to feel the scorpion scourge
Of torture from my bosom purge
My sin, so that, all worn and broken,
Shattered by pains no tongue hath spoken,
With guiltless soul I may emerge
As when I played, a little child,
And kissed my mother as she smiled.
I would with fierce crusading bands
Invade the burning Paynim lands,
And shed my blood on parching sands.
Or else a hermit I would be
Beside some stormy northern sea,
And feed like beasts upon the roots
I'd gather there and bitter fruits,
Praying for death to set me free
From life's enduring agony.
And if I could believe that so,
In living like the olden saints,
I could wash off the guilt that taints
My soul, I forth would gladly go.

PRIEST.

My son, those saints obtained remission
Of sin, who fasted, wept and prayed,
Lashing their backs in deep contrition,
God's mercy seeking and His aid.
Penance is holy, and the yearning
So fiercely in thy bosom burning

God plants to teach thee how to win
Forgiveness for thy grievous sin.

SEBASTIAN.

I would, my father, I might share
Thy faith, but that long since is past.
How gladly would I pray and fast
Could I believe forgiveness there.
No, not in useless penance shall I find
The balm for my distracted mind.
If right the voice of conscience speaks,
'Tis not the selfish saint who seeks
Alone his own salvation who
The path of duty doth pursue.
Not through the desert doth it lie,
But through the busy haunts of men,
Where we must walk with pitying eye,
Prepared to lend assistance when
We hear the voice of sorrow call.
Not in the shade of cloister wall,
Trying to save our souls alone
For errors past do we atone.
'Tis in the tumult and the strife,
The agony of human life,
Doing our duty unto all,
Fighting the battles of the weak,
Wiping the tear from Sorrow's cheek,
Warring for right against the wrong,

'Tis thus we should our pardon seek.
Such was the life my father led,
And in his steps I'll feebly tread.
And here between the honored dead,
The one so fair, the one so strong —
The one who beckons me to heaven,
Who heaven's own bliss to me has given,
The other who has shown me where
The path of human duty leads —
Even here I dedicate my life
To comforting the heart that bleeds,
To raising souls from their despair,
To duty's path of pain and strife.
The way is long, but when I falter
I'll turn to those who slumber here,
And kneeling as beside an altar,
Fresh strength I'll find my heart to cheer.

PRIEST.

My son, I mourn thy want of faith,
But follow on in Virtue's path,
And God the phials of His wrath
May still withhold, and ere thy death
Thou mayst His blessed mercy feel,
And at His shrine repentant kneel.
Then will the peace no tongue can tell
Abide with thee.   My son, farewell.